DICING WITH DEATH

BETH CHAMBERS

ILLUSTRATED BY

WARWICK JOHNSON-CADWELL

A &
AN IMPRINT
LONDON NEW DELHI

CONTENTS

CHAPTER ONE

'**M**ummeeee!' Amy screamed.

Max winced. His little sister had the ability to reach a glass-shattering decibel level.

Amy stood in the doorway, her mouth open, her eyes wide.

There were bits of doll everywhere. A severed head swung gently from the light shade.

Max snapped his fingers at their dog Toby, who was playing catch with a plastic leg. Toby ignored Max completely and trotted over to Amy. Saliva drooled from his mouth as he proudly spat out the torso of a well-chewed doll.

Max covered his ears as Amy gave another scream. This one wouldn't stop at shattering glass – it could probably bring down entire buildings.

'I'm telling Mum!' Amy stamped hard on Max's foot and marched out of the door. Max didn't bother going after her. He knew without fail that he would get the blame for Toby sneaking into Amy's room and decimating her dolls. Whatever he said, his mother would take Amy's side.

Max was more wound up about it than usual because so far he'd babysat every day of the Christmas holidays.

A door banged somewhere downstairs.

'Maximus, you get down these stairs right now.' His mother sounded beyond annoyed. 'I've only got a half-hour lunch break. I'm going to be late back to work. The last thing I need is you winding up your sister!'

Max ran his fingers through his short black hair to flatten the spikes that had a mind of their own. He had a quick peek in the mirror to check that he was wearing his most innocent expression. He had a range of them – this one was called, *Who me? Never!*

Twenty minutes later Max headed down the street with Amy in tow. His sister had refused to go anywhere near Toby since the doll incident, so he'd had to leave the dog at home. He walked quickly, knowing that Amy's little legs would have to jog to keep up.

'What's the matter, Max?' Amy called.

'Everything,' he said shortly.

Angry thoughts zoomed around his head. He could pinpoint exactly when everything had started to go wrong. It had been seven years ago, when his dad had walked out.

No, slunk out, Max thought, kicking a stone, *and not just down the road. Ooh nooo. Dad's got to head off to New Zealand on my fifth birthday. While I'm at Nan's blowing out candles, he's at home, packing his bags and blowing out his family.*

Max had only ever seen his mother cry once, and that was when she had read the note his dad had left on the kitchen table. After that she had put on a brave, although frequently stressed, face, and they had got along just fine.

That was before she had met David.

'Where we going, Max?' Amy tugged on his coat.

'The woods,' he muttered.

'Can I go piggy bank?' she continued, undaunted by his mood.

'I told you before, it's called a piggy back,' snapped Max.

'Can I go piggy back then?'

'No.' But he slowed down so that she no longer had to jog to keep up.

He had been seven when David had barged into their lives. By the time he was nine his mother had married David and, if that wasn't bad enough, delivered Amy as a small, mewling rug-rat.

Reaching the end of the street Max squeezed through a hole in some old fencing and scrambled down an overgrown bank into the forest. He turned to wait while Amy slowly inched her way through the gap.

'Hurry up,' he urged as she caught her pink jacket on a splinter.

'Max, it's torn!' she wailed.

'No it's not. Look, if I just snap the thread like this...' he began. What had been a small snag in the sleeve suddenly became a hole large enough to wiggle his finger in.

Amy shrieked.

Max hid a grin. 'Whoops!'

'I want to go to the den.' Amy sniffed.

Max pretended not to hear. He turned and crunched along the pine needle strewn path. The den was his private place. He'd built it deep in the forest where no one else would find it. Recently he had taken a plastic milk crate down there to use as a table. Surprise, surprise, it had been another babysitting day, and he had made the fatal mistake of taking Amy with him. Since then all she had done was nag him to take her back.

'I'm not taking you. We're going to the lake instead,' Max told her.

'Why?'

'I'm going to get myself one of the trees planted there.'

'Why?'

'Because this Christmas I'm having my own tree in my own room.'

'Why?'

'Because this Christmas,' Max said, rubbing his hands up and down his arms to keep warm, 'I'm spending on my own. No Mum, no David…'

'No Amy?' Amy said in a small voice.

'And no Amy,' Max said firmly. 'This Christmas is going to be family-free.'

CHAPTER TWO

'Will you still get presents from Father Christmas?' Amy pouted, looking upset.

Max stared at her. 'What?' he snapped. Not looking where he was going, his foot suddenly sank into something mushy, steaming and very smelly. 'Shhh...ugar!'

He did his best to scrape his trainer clean while ignoring Amy's giggles. By the time they had reached the lake, Max could cheerfully have thrown her in. Knowing that he might have a question or two to answer at home if he did, instead he picked up a pebble and skimmed it across the black expanse of water. His real dad had taught him how to snap back his wrist and send the pebble scudding across the surface. He'd taught him other things too, like how to make bows and arrows, how to belch the national anthem and how to produce the most awesome farting sounds from under his armpit. He'd been a great dad. Not like David with his, 'Tidy your room, Max,' and 'Let's work out a payment plan for this broken window, Max.'

Deep down, Max *knew* that his real dad was going to come back. *He would have come back aeons ago if Mum hadn't been so quick to remarry*, he fumed, kicking some loose pebbles into the water.

'Max?' Amy tugged at his sleeve. 'I'm getting cold.'

Max glued a vacant smile to his face. 'You can help me look for a tree. That will warm you up.'

'OK.' Amy pushed her hair out of her eyes and gazed around at the towering pines that dominated the landscape like giant forest guardians. She tugged off her gloves.

'You'd best keep them on,' Max told her, 'you'll freeze without them. Your fingers will turn into icicles and they'll snap off.'

Amy tramped off towards the nearest line of trees while Max headed off in the opposite direction. Moments later he heard his sister shriek.

'Max, Max, I found the best tree ever!'

Max hurried around the mouth of the lake and found Amy standing with her arms wrapped around a tree at least three times her size. 'That's not a tree, that's a forest! Look, Amy, they've planted the smaller trees closer to the lake. Look there, OK?'

'Is it bad to take them?' Amy whispered. 'Dad says stealing is wrong.'

'It's only *bad* if we get caught.' Max winked.

'You'll be in big trouble.'

'No, I won't.'

'Will.'

Max blew out a long breath, sending a column of hot steam into the freezing air. 'No I *won't*, because I've been looking after you all holiday and the forest fairies have decided I deserve a reward.'

'Forest fairies!' Amy's eyes widened.

'Yep. They're all over the place, watching everything you do. If you're good they give you a present, but if you're bad they punish you.'

'How?' Amy was hanging on his every word.

'They play mean tricks on you. Sometimes they'll follow you home and wait until it's dark and you're asleep. Then they creep into your bedroom and steal all of your teeth.'

'I don't believe you,' Amy said flatly.

Max was impressed. Perhaps his baby sister was finally starting to grow up.

But she went on, 'Fairies wouldn't play nasty tricks on you. Everyone knows fairies are kind.

14

They only take your teeth if you leave them under the pillow an' then they put money out for you.'

Max shook his head and rolled his eyes. 'Forget it!' He stamped his feet on the ground to warm them up before returning his attention to tree hunting. He stomped off into the forest, breathing in the sweet smell of pine.

Suddenly he saw just the one. It was a little taller than he was and bushy without sprouting untidily all over the place. Bingo!

Max flipped open his pocket knife and pulled out the largest of the blades. Carefully he began to saw.

Ten minutes later he was still sawing and his arm was burning like it was about to spontaneously combust. He kicked the tree in frustration.

Infuriatingly, it barely trembled.

At that moment, he became aware of a strange stillness in the forest. He couldn't shake the feeling that he was being watched. The hairs on the back of his neck prickled.

'Amy?' he called.

The glade suddenly didn't feel safe. There was something creepy lurking in the air.

'Amy, is that you?' he called again, peering through the trees.

She didn't reply. Where was she?

Max pocketed his knife and hurried back towards the lake. The lake! What if Amy had fallen in? She was only five. She couldn't swim without her armbands. Max broke into a sprint, twisting and turning to avoid crashing into trees.

Bursting through the bushes at the lakeside, Max imagined Amy's pink jacket swollen with water and her small body face down in the water, her blonde hair streaming around her.

He stared up and down the length of the lake.

She wasn't there.

Max took deep gasps of relief before yelling out her name in a long-drawn-out cry.

Flapping their wings, a flock of birds flew up into the air, startled from where they had been roosting in the treetops.

But there was no responding shout from his sister.

Max had to face it.

Amy was missing.

CHAPTER THREE

While Max pounded along the path toward his house, horrible thoughts forced their way into his head. What if Amy had fallen into the lake and had got all tangled up in the weeds? *Why did I leave her on her own?*

Out of the corner of his eye he saw a bright flash appear through the trees. A moment later there was a second brilliant gleam of light. Something was lurking in the forest, keeping pace with him.

'Who's there?' he yelled.

He strained his ears but heard nothing but silence.

Reaching the bank Max scrambled up it and squeezed through the fence. He quickly scanned the street.

Nothing.

It took Max three attempts to fit the key into his front door. Finally it turned and he stepped into the hall. Picking up the phone, he punched in his mother's mobile number.

'Hello?' She sounded annoyed already.

'Mum...'

'Max. I hope you've got a good reason for ringing. I'm in the middle of a meeting.'

'Amy's missing,' Max choked.

'What do you mean? What's wrong?'

'Mum... I've lost her.' His throat tightened and his voice went wobbly.

'Where?' his mother snapped.

Quickly Max told her what had happened.

'Right, phone the police and tell them what's happened. I'm on my way home. Call 999, now!' his mother rapped, machine-gun-style, and then hung up.

* * *

His mother and David arrived at exactly the same moment, bursting through the front door together.

Max had never seen his mother look so chalk-coloured. As for David... he actually looked worried. Not once in the last six years had Max seen David's face a degree over *concerned*. Broken windows, flaming rows, detentions, irate teachers and broken curfews had all been tackled by Mr Calm and Capable himself. Looking at this new anxious stepfather, Max suddenly wanted the old one back.

'I'm so sorry, Mum. I didn't mean to lose her, honest.'

His mother stared at him with cold blue eyes.

'It's all right, we know you didn't.' David filled the awkward silence.

Max's mother rounded on David. 'Anything could have happened to Amy! She could be lying dead at the bottom of the lake, or have been abducted… and what are we doing? Sitting on our backsides doing nothing, that's what!'

She slammed into the living room.

'She doesn't blame you,' David said gently.

'What do you know?' Max shouted. 'Everything was fine until you came along. None of this would be happening if Mum hadn't met you, because there wouldn't *be* an Amy. It would just be the two of us, like before. I hate you! I wish you'd disappear too!' His voice trailed off as two police officers walked in through the open front door.

David's mouth opened and closed like a goldfish before he hustled the police into the living room and firmly closed the door.

Minutes ticked by until Max couldn't bear the suspense of waiting any more. He pressed his ear against the door and listened to his mother speaking.

'I just don't understand why you're so interested in Max. He's a good boy. He wouldn't do anything to hurt Amy.'

'In all likelihood your daughter has just wandered off and is lost, but given the circumstances, we have to establish whether there are any problems concerning family relationships. It may surprise you to know that in situations such as these it's often a close family member who is involved,' came the reply.

Max felt sick. They were more or less accusing him of having done something to Amy!

Without waiting to hear more, Max tore out of the house and raced into the rapidly gathering dark, only to stumble over the uneven paving slabs. Lying face down he lashed out with his fists in frustration, grazing all of his knuckles in the process. It didn't make him feel any better, but he did it again anyway.

I shouldn't have run, said a voice in his head. *All I've done is made myself look one hundred per cent guilty.*

The police had probably already passed his details on to the rest of the force branding him as a wanted criminal: highly dangerous, approach with caution. Well, he wouldn't go home until he had searched the whole of the forest and found Amy. His den – that was the first place he should look.

Max hurried along the frozen track, running as fast as he dared in the dark. Every snapping twig sounded like a pistol crack. He swerved off the track at roughly the point where he guessed his den was and held out his hands to feel his way. Pictures from horror movies forced their way into his mind, until he became convinced that behind every tree lurked hideous monsters.

He crashed into a small bush and furiously fought off the freezing, finger-like branches before rolling away. He didn't bother getting back up but stayed on his hands and knees, crawling in what he hoped was the right direction. Finally his hands felt mud instead of prickly pine needles.

He was on the path that led to his den.

Max scrambled down the twisting track that led into the tar black glade. 'Amy!' His voice rang out. 'It's Max. I've come to get you. Amy, where are you?'

He was greeted with silence. Disappointment rushed over him. *She's not here.* He sank onto the mossy ground and shivered with cold.

Once again he began to sense he wasn't alone. He gazed into the thick blackness. 'Who's there?'

A glowing silver arc appeared in the distance. Max screwed up his eyes and realised it was bobbing towards him through the air.

The object came to a halt just in front of him. Max's breathing came fast and hard. It was the blade of a scythe. He scrambled up, wanting to run, but his feet were like two blocks of concrete.

With a faint swish, a dark hood fell back to reveal the side profile of a face. No, not a face...

Max staggered back a few steps as a skull of gleaming ivory swung around towards him.

There was a seven-foot skeleton staring down at him.

It was the Grim Reaper.

CHAPTER FOUR

Max stared into Death's eyes – well, his eye sockets – until the distance between Max and the Grim Reaper appeared to lengthen. The skeleton's ivory features blurred as he floated away. This was the time to make a run for it.

Then Max saw what Death was moving towards.

The Grim Reaper raised his scythe, and from it spilled an eerie blue light that trickled down onto a small, crumpled pink bundle.

'Oh, no,' Max whispered.

His sister was curled up in a tangle of undergrowth.

Max desperately wanted to race over to Amy but running towards her also meant running towards Death.

The Grim Reaper looked across at him and appeared to grin. With two bony hands he brought down the long-handled scythe.

Max bolted forward as the blade sliced down like a guillotine. Launching himself off the ground, he threw himself across Amy's lifeless body. 'No!' he screamed. 'You can't have her!'

Max waited for the slice of cold steel against his neck. Amy lay unmoving in his arms. Time ticked by, and still his head was safely attached to his body. Daringly, he squinted upwards. The Grim Reaper had vanished.

Max turned his attention to Amy. 'Please don't let her be dead,' he whispered, stripping off his coat and tucking it around her. Amy's face was as white as one of her china dolls and her lips were purplish blue – the same colour she had been just minutes after she was born. David had called him into the hospital room where his mum was lying with Amy in her arms. 'Say hello to your new baby sister,' she'd smiled, dropping a kiss onto Amy's head. Max had felt a sharp jab of jealousy. 'Half-sister,' he had pointed out.

For the first time in five years, Max felt uncomfortable with the way he'd acted that day.

'Amy,' he urged. 'Come on, open your eyes.'

Gradually it dawned on him that not only could he see Amy, but that she was lying in a pool of light. Glancing up he saw the source of the light was the scythe. Death hadn't gone at all, he had simply moved further away.

The Grim Reaper regarded him, skull tilted to one side. 'Enough!' His voice reverberated like a tomb slamming closed. 'It is time. Your sister must leave this world.'

Something deep and angry inside Max began to boil. He leapt to his feet. 'You can't take her,' he screamed with clenched fists. 'I won't let you.'

With only a skull for a face, Death wasn't naturally good at expressions, but despite this Max got the impression the Grim Reaper didn't like being defied by a mortal. 'Don't be foolish,' he boomed. 'Move out of the way.'

'I don't think so,' Max croaked.

Death tipped his head back, almost as if he were laughing, and appeared to take a huge breath. Then he dropped his head again, opened his jaw and released a howling blast of freezing air.

The force of the surge knocked Max off his feet and propelled him half way across the glade. He slammed against a tree trunk, the sudden pain in his back fighting for supremacy with the agony in his ears as roaring wind tore through the forest.

A giant hourglass appeared in the air above Amy. Death appeared to be waiting for the last of the sand to run from the top bulb to the bottom. A gold thread shimmered between the hourglass and Amy's heart. Max gulped. It was Amy's lifeline.

Once again, Death raised his scythe into the air.

It was at this precise moment that inspiration hit Max like an icy wave.

'Stop! Stop! I'll play you!' he shouted.

For a long moment, nothing moved. Death remained with his arms raised, about to sever Amy's lifeline; Max lay against the tree where he'd landed, hardly daring to breathe.

Slowly, Death lowered his scythe.

'What?' His deep voice boomed around the glade.

'That's the rule, right? I can challenge you to a game. Everybody knows that,' Max gabbled. 'I'm allowed to play a game with you, and if I win you can't take Amy.'

Death floated slowly across the forest floor towards Max. The way he moved had the uncanny effect of making the forest seem as if it were rushing into the distance, while Death himself stayed perfectly still. Max screwed up his eyes as the world shifted and bent out of focus.

'Actually,' said Death, leaning over him, 'it's the best of three.'

CHAPTER FIVE

'If you choose to join the queue of candidates, you will have a very long wait,' grinned Death.

'W-w-what?' stuttered Max, before his brain clicked into gear. He could put up with a day or two's wait. This was for Amy's life, he'd queue for weeks if need be. 'What will happen to Amy while I'm waiting?' he panted. 'She'll be alright, won't she?'

'What she will be,' boomed Death 'is old. The queue is thirty years long, give or take a month or two.'

Max's eyes widened. 'Thirty years!'

Death swung his scythe so that its sharp blade pointed forward like the beak of a bird of prey. Realising what was about to happen, Max rolled sideways as the huge blade fell, missing him by millimetres and slicing into the stony ground. A crack appeared which rapidly grew deeper and wider. Stones rattled down into the depths of what had suddenly become a chasm, before two podgy grey hands appeared on either side of the crack. These were followed by a face more wrinkled than a British bulldog with hairy warts sprouting on the folds of grey skin. The creature had long pointed ears, a beaky, sharp nose and slanting, luminous eyes. Accompanying his struggle through the gap was a sound like a balloon being deflated. This was immediately followed by the smell of rotten eggs.

'Whoops,' the creature smirked. 'Pardon me.'

'Mopsus,' Death sighed.

The creature called Mopsus was only about three feet tall, but he was able to reach eye level with Death thanks to the madly flapping feathered wings attached to his ankles.

'Master Reaper.' His voice grated like two stones being ground together.

Death dipped his head slightly. 'This... *boy* has challenged me to a game.'

Mopsus scratched his head. 'Another one? I don't know where you expect me to put him. They're queueing back as far as the boiler room. Tempers are getting pretty hot down there.' He coughed, splattering Max with stinking phlegm. 'Ahem, no pun intended.'

Death leaned a little closer to Mopsus. 'Perhaps you might suggest an alternative,' he intoned. 'The boy should be given the chance to save his sister, no matter how slight. I believe we have an *understanding*?' He emphasised the last word so that it echoed around the glade.

Mopsus glanced in Max's direction, comprehension flitting across his ugly face. 'Oh,' he said haughtily. 'Yes, of course. I suppose the boy could be *my* assistant. After all, being your personal assistant is an immensely time-consuming job, and I really could use a new minion to clean up after the zombies – perhaps sew back on the occasional limb. And then there are the ghouls – they're forever haunting places where they have no right to be. I just hope he's a bit more hardy than the last one you gave me. He was in pieces before the week was out. Literally.' He scowled. 'Perhaps we could come to some arrangement with... er...'

'Max,' Max supplied.

'Yes, Max, to take on a short-term contract in return for Amy's life?'

'Eh?' Max was struggling to keep up. Why did they want him when there was a thirty-year-long queue of candidates to choose from? It didn't make any sense. His glance slid to Amy. Now wasn't the time for looking a gift horse in its mouth – or in this case, a gift skeleton and its hideous PA.

'I'll do it on one condition,' Max began, trying to sound more confident than he felt. 'Amy goes home – *now*.'

32

'Boy, making demands is really not the best way to start off your working relationship with me,' Mopsus spat with a sly sidelong glance at Death.

Death spoke over him. 'Max will be *my* assistant. Not yours. Take the girl to her parents' house, Mopsus.'

Mopsus's mouth dropped open. Max saw several maggots squirming around the gaps in the creature's rotten teeth. 'But *I'm* your – '

'Enough!' Death scowled. 'Take the girl back. Now!'

Mopsus glared at Max who felt completely bemused. He was going to be working for Death, *directly*? He hoped he wouldn't have to kill anyone.

'Of course,' rumbled Death, 'if you do not fulfil your contract with me I will come back for your sister and her life will not be the only one to be forfeit – yours is also on the line.' He stretched out his scythe and pressed it against Max's chest.

Max gulped. Questions raced through his mind. How short was the 'short' in his contract? What precisely would his job description be, since Mopsus clearly thought of himself as Death's personal assistant? And how had Mopsus known Amy's name?

Before he could voice any of them, Death snapped his fingers, and a moment later Max heard a gentle splash. Losing his balance, he collapsed onto a wooden seat and felt the motion of a boat gliding through water. Max faced the stern, but could only just make it out through the swirling thick fog.

'I thought we would take the scenic route.' Death's voice rumbled. 'If you are to be my assistant, you will need to learn your way around my kingdom. Take the key. It is next to you.'

'Why?' Max questioned as his fingers connected with smooth, cold brass.

'Do not lose it,' Death went on, ignoring him. 'Without it you cannot gain entrance to, or exit from, the Underworld.'

Exit sounds good, Max thought. *It's entrance I'm not so keen on.*

A faint high-pitched howling sounded. It was the type of noise that made you think of werewolves and haunted graveyards. Worse, they seemed to be floating closer and closer to it.

'What's that?' asked Max.

'Cerberus.'

'Cerberus?' Max grew uncomfortably aware of a smell worse than a crate full of rotting rats.

34

'I would not do that if I were you,' Death said, as Max peered intently into the gloom. 'Those who look Cerberus in the eye turn to stone.'

'What?' yelled Max, squeezing his eyes shut and pulling his jumper over his head.

'He is the guardian of the entrance to Hades – my Underworld. Show him the key.'

Max raised a shaking hand.

'Not to that head – it's not looking at you.'

'W-w-what d'you mean, not *that* head?' Max panicked. 'How many heads does it have?'

'Three. Unless you count the snake, and then it would be four.'

'The snake?' Max repeated, while transferring the key into his other hand and waving it madly.

'Cerberus's tail. It is very effective at keeping uninvited people out,' Death replied.

Max couldn't imagine there were that many people trying to get in.

They carried on down the river. As the panting and snarling faded, Max risked opening his eyes to narrow slits. The craggy rocks that rose up on either side of the river were illuminated by burning torches. Against the fiery backdrop, he saw the shadow of a creature larger than an elephant straddling the river. Each of its three massive heads had wide-open jaws, revealing teeth like razor-sharp tombstones.

What am I doing? Max panicked, quickly squeezing his eyes shut again.

Suddenly, the boat bumped into a stone ledge and stopped. Opening his eyes, Max saw that they had floated into a low-roofed cave. He scrambled after Death, who turned and plucked the key from Max's hand before leading the way to a huge room made from great slabs of black marble. The floor, walls and roof were all made of the smooth, glistening stone, making Max feel like he was trapped in an enormous, stickerless Rubik's Cube. The light from the flickering torches threw Death's shadow against the walls as he stalked towards an ornately carved table.

Mopsus was waiting for them.

'Don't tell me, you took the scenic route?' Mopsus said knowingly while Death took his seat at the head of the table.

Scenic isn't exactly the first word that comes to mind, thought Max, as Death indicated he should sit down.

Mopsus heaved his fat body over to Max's side of the table, and slid a tightly rolled-up scroll towards him.

Death snapped his fingers and the scroll unrolled.

Max peered intently at the spidery writing but he couldn't make any sense out of it. There was an empty, thick red line at the bottom of the parchment.

'Sign.' Death leaned over to tap the parchment with a long bony finger. 'Now.'

'I can't read it. What does it say?' Max asked nervously.

'That you agree to become Death's assistant for a non-specified period of time,' interrupted Mopsus, speaking with such speed that Max could barely follow what he was saying. 'That once you have signed you cannot change your mind and ask to go home. That you cannot sue if you are injured, lose any of your limbs or die during the course of your employment. Oh, and that if you fail in any of your duties, not only will your own life be forfeit but Death will claim your sister's soul. Now *sign*.'

Max felt a spasm of fear shoot up his spine. 'Alright.' He nodded. He felt a sudden rush of daring. 'But where does *Death* sign?'

'Pardon?' said Mopsus, quietly.

'Where does Death sign to agree that Amy and I are free once I'm done?'

'I?' boomed Death. 'Sign?' Swirls of acrid smoke wafted from his eye sockets.

Max's courage buckled. Hastily he grabbed the black-feathered quill that appeared from thin air. The nib made a loud scratching noise whilst oozing out thick red ink. He had barely finished the last letter of his name when the scroll rolled itself up and vanished.

How, Max wondered, had the contract been drawn up so quickly? Had he been expected?

Before he had time to brood any further, Death lifted his hand from his chair's skull-studded armrest. 'The kitchen is through that door.' He pointed. 'You may fetch refreshments.'

Surprised that Death had something as mundane as a kitchen, Max got up and made his way across the hall. Before he reached the door he stopped and looked over shoulder. 'My mother…' He hesitated. 'She'll be worried about me. She'll think I've run away.'

Death dipped his head in acknowledgement. 'Maximus Di Angelo,' he intoned. 'You are about to become a statistic.'

CHAPTER SIX

Death's kitchen had the spiders' webs and gloomy lighting that seemed a pre-requisite in the Underworld. Unlike the great hall, which was cavernous, the kitchen was cosy by comparison, although it was still bigger than the entire downstairs of Max's house. Shelves hewn out of black marble were crowded with plates, bowls and goblets. *What does he need all this stuff for?* It wasn't as if Death could eat or drink – it would leak through the gaps that were supposed to be plugged by flesh and sinew.

The best description for Death's kitchen was 'random' – as if it had been built by someone who had never boiled an egg in his life, but had raided a stash of *Good Housekeeping* magazines. Black marble counters rose up in various places, strung about with chintz curtains. Copper pots and pans were suspended from a huge chain strung across the ceiling. Max couldn't see an oven and assumed that any cooking took place over the small fire that smoked in an open fireplace.

'What are you doing here?' snapped a high-pitched voice. 'Nobody dead is allowed in Death's private quarters.'

'I'm not dead!' Max span around and saw a girl who looked only a little older than himself. Her long red hair tumbled untidily over her shoulders and her green eyes were piercing.

She put her hands on her hips. 'Well then, you're *definitely* in the wrong place.'

'I know. Apparently I'm Death's new personal assistant,' Max said gloomily.

'But Mopsus is his PA!'

'I think I must be the other one.'

'The other one?'

'Never mind.' Max didn't understand it either. 'Death sent me in for refreshments.'

She sighed. 'Food doesn't appear like magic in this place, you know.'

'Erm…' squirmed Max, feeling awkward, as he realised she must be the cook. 'What's old Bone Face like then, you know, as a boss?' He was feeling a little braver now that a door separated him from the Grim Reaper.

'You don't want to let him hear you calling him that. He's very hit and miss when it comes to humour,' the girl replied, frowning. 'Since you have a problem with names, let me spell mine out for you. It's L I A H.'

Adopting one of his most sincerely innocent faces, Max mangled the pronunciation just to get a rise out of her. 'Liar! That's an interesting name.'

'You're not funny.'

Max held up his hands. 'OK, sorry. Liah, as in the princess from *Star Wars*?'

'What are you talking about?' Liah pulled back one of the hideous floral curtains and took out a round loaf of bread that looked as if it could be entered into a shot put contest.

Max suspected a chainsaw would be of more use than the blunt knife she was using to hack off a slice. 'You've never heard of *Star Wars*?' he said, surprised. 'How long have you been down here?'

'Some of us don't have time to sit around talking. You could help.' Liah indicated a pot beside the sorry excuse for a fire. 'That needs to be put on to heat.'

Max picked up the pot and hung it on a giant hook over the flames. He lifted the lid and his stomach rebelled at the sight and smell of the thick grey contents. Occasionally something solid would bubble up to the surface only to be dragged back beneath the thick skin of the liquid, possibly by something still alive. Max backed away from the pungent aroma, focusing all his energy on not being sick, before he realised that Liah was talking.

'What?'

'You haven't been listening,' she huffed. 'I was saying that down here, it's impossible to keep track of time. No one ages either. I'm sure I've been here for at least a year. One thing I'm certain of,' she said darkly, 'is that I'm owed leave.' She reached up to retrieve plates and goblets.

'So you're not dead then?'

'Do I look dead?' she snapped.

Max hesitated. To be quite honest she did look a bit ghostlike with her alabaster skin and large eyes. Her floral apron spoilt the overall supernatural effect, but give Liah a white sheet and she'd be more than convincing.

'Well?' she prompted.

'You do look as if a touch of sun wouldn't be a bad thing,' Max said, evading the question. He looked at her thin frame and decided not to mention the fact that she also looked in need of a good meal. Girls could be so touchy about their weight.

Liah poured water into two goblets. 'I can't remember what it's like to feel the sun on my skin.' She sounded wistful.

'So if you're not dead, how did you end up here?'

Liah's lips pressed into a thin line. 'I played Death and lost, but instead of taking my life he offered me a job. His cook had just quit – some row about his talent being wasted – and Death said I could become his housekeeper instead of having my soul harvested.' She sighed. 'I'm still not convinced I made the right choice.'

Max waited for her to load up the tray. 'Do you want me to carry it through?'

She hesitated then thrust the tray into his hands.

Max looked down at the bowls of unappetising grey sludge. 'Um, thanks?'

'Whatever.' She turned on her heel and disappeared into the darker recesses of the kitchen.

Mopsus looked up when Max kicked open the door. 'Ah, yet more culinary delights from the lovely Liah,' he purred mischievously.

Setting down the tray on the table, Max attempted to eat a piece of bread. He gave up when his teeth starting making ominous cracking noises.

Candelabras had been lit and their light played over Death's polished skull.

'It is time for your first test.' Death leaned back in his seat and regarded Max.

'Test?' Max echoed in surprise.

'Task,' Mopsus smoothly interjected. 'I'm sure you'll have no problems completing it. After all, you are Death's PA now.'

Max narrowed his eyes. He wondered if Mopsus always sounded as if his vocal chords had been liberally coated with sarcasm. 'So.' Max tried to speak casually. 'What is this task?' He waited to be told that he had to go wrestle a ten-headed dragon or face an army of the undead.

'You are to go and collect your robes,' Death told him.

'That's it?'

'You sound disappointed.' Mopsus waggled his bushy eyebrows. 'Did you want to do something more… *challenging*?'

'No,' Max said quickly. 'Picking up clothes is fine by me. Where are they? The laundry?'

Mopsus grinned, revealing his uneven yellow teeth. 'Not exactly.'

CHAPTER SEVEN

'So where do I go?' Max asked. He followed Mopsus down a flight of glistening stone steps that led to a small jetty. Bobbing gently on a black ribbon of water, a small rowing boat awaited them.

'It's probably better you don't know.' Mopsus paused to reach around and scratch under his loincloth.

'Did you just sniff your fingers?' Max screwed up his face. Talk about an overload of gross!

Mopsus ignored the question. 'No one would blame you if you wanted to quit. There are less painful ways to die than working as *his* assistant. All you have to do is tell *him* you want out – at least that way you'll spare yourself the next rather gory hour or so.'

'Thanks, but I'm planning on staying alive,' Max snapped. His stomach twisted with nerves.

How difficult was the task going to be? Was it some sort of initiation – trial by robe? He recalled what Death had said earlier – that if Max failed in any of his tasks, his life would be forfeit. And Amy's.

Mopsus shrugged. 'Suit yourself. I was just trying to offer you a nice easy ending rather than a painful, drawn-out – '

'Yes, OK, I get the picture.' Max's lips tightened into a thin line.

Mopsus turned around and stared, his eyes gleaming in the light of the lantern he was holding. 'I don't think you do. *No one* escapes Death once they're in *his* hands.' He allowed the words to hang in the air before turning and stepping on to the jetty.

Max's fingers dug in to his palms. He had to believe that Death would keep his word. *I'm going to totally smash every task he gives me so Amy and I stay alive*, he thought desperately. *I will. I have to.*

'This one's for the catacombs,' Mopsus announced to the shrouded figure in the middle of the boat. No part of the boatman was visible under the shroud apart from his gnarled hands, which ended in long twisted fingernails that were a colour somewhere between yellow and pea green.

Trying not to show that he was shaken by Mopsus's threat, Max climbed in and positioned himself at the far end. With a faint splash the boat eased away and the hideous form of Mopsus was soon lost from sight, swallowed up by the gloom.

The only sound in the tunnel was the quiet splash of the oars. Sitting in the dark, it was hard to judge how much time had passed before the surroundings opened out to reveal a vast underground lake. In the centre was a small island. When the boat came to a stop Max looked around for a landing stage, then realised he was expected to jump into the water. 'You've got to be kidding me,' he muttered.

A low moan rose from the depths of the boatman's shroud.

Hastily, Max kicked off his shoes and leapt out. Freezing water soaked him to the skin as he half-swam, half-waded to the shore. He debated whether or not to strip off the wet material that clung to his flesh, but then pictured himself wandering the catacombs in his pants.

Just. No.

Max began to crunch over what he thought were bleached white sticks and pebbles, until he stepped on what was undeniably a human jaw bone. *What is this place?* The hairs on the back of his neck prickled as he scanned the landscape. Everywhere he looked was pure white. Bone white.

A short distance away stood two upright black stones that supported a smaller slab, marking the entrance to a tunnel. Figuring that this must be the entrance to the catacombs, Max crunched his way over what he now desperately wished were sticks and pebbles, and stepped inside. Ahead of him lay a sloping passage leading underground. Cold damp crept over Max as he made his way along the tunnel that ended in a steep flight of steps.

Down in the bowels of the catacombs was a maze of crumbling walls. Holes had been gouged out of them, creating the appearance of a giant honeycomb. Max placed his hand on one of the chalky walls before curiously peering into a recess. It wasn't just a hole, it was a tunnel. His eyes slowly adjusted to the dark, and he shouted out with fright.

Shuffling through the gloom, heading straight towards him, was a zombie. Its skin hung loosely as if it didn't quite fit its skeleton. Milky white eyes stared ahead sightlessly, while mumbling groans escaped its dry, cracked lips.

Max whipped his head out of the recess and flattened himself back against the main tunnel wall, his heart pounding. What kind of place was this? The creature stopped in the entrance to what

Max could only assume was its burrow. *Turn right*, Max prayed, fear pinning him to the spot. *Please, please don't look my way.*

The creature turned left.

It drew level with Max and stopped before slowly turning its head. Opening its mouth, it expelled a sigh of foul air. The stench of death and decay was overpowering. Its limbs twitched and convulsed as it slowly raised its hands, ready to attack.

Max slid down the wall until he was crouched at the creature's rotting feet. Luckily for him, this particular zombie didn't seem to be particularly quick off the mark. Fighting back the urge to be sick, he crawled as rapidly as he could in the opposite direction, towards the centre of the catacombs.

Realising its prey had escaped, the zombie gave a long drawn-out cry, which was soon answered by similar moans from the hundreds of other burrows within the walls.

Great, thought Max. Outfoxing one zombie was fine, but fighting a whole army of them was another matter. What would they do to him? Would he become one of them, or would they eat his brains and throw his body outside to crumble along with the other bones?

His breath came in long painful gasps as he tore along the corridor, the shuffling of feet growing ever closer as the zombies joined the main passageway.

A faint draught blew against his cheek and instinctively he turned towards the first hint of fresh air he'd felt since descending into this hellhole. He followed the steady stream of air down a narrow twisting tunnel until finally he reached a solid wooden door that barred his way. Fumbling in his pocket for the key he had shown Cerberus, Max suddenly remembered that Death had taken it away. He was trapped!

He scrabbled desperately at the lock, rattling the door handle and pushing with all his might, but it was no use. The door wouldn't budge. Behind him, the moans of the zombies grew louder.

His very first task and he had failed. He closed his eyes and leaned his forehead against the door. 'I'm sorry, Amy,' he whispered. Amy would die, and he was going to be torn to pieces. Unless…

Max grabbed the door handle, twisted it, and pulled.

With the slightest of creaks, the door swung open towards him. It wasn't locked after all. It just opened outwards.

Max staggered forward in relief and fell onto a sandy floor. Whipping round, he caught a glimpse of a crowd of zombies stumbling towards him. Instantly, he yanked the door closed and dropped the wooden plank that served as a bolt into place. 'Note to self, never assume an escape route is locked when being chased by an army of zombies,' he panted. And as an afterthought, 'Some doors you have to pull, not push.'

Ignoring the angry thuds and moans from other side of the door, Max turned to check out his new surroundings. He was in a huge oval arena. High walls enclosed the sandy grounds, while towering rows of stone seats rose in tiers all around. It appeared to be the ruins of a once great amphitheatre. Scattered throughout the arena stood a collection of stone pillars, each holding an item of treasure. Max's gaze raked over elaborate suits of armour, coffers of gold coins, haunting statues and glittering jewels until he found what he was looking for. In the very centre, on a tall stone column, was a neatly folded mustard-coloured robe.

Max looked all around. Satisfied he was alone, he hurried to the middle of the arena and jumped up and down until he managed to grab a corner of the robe. He pulled it down and with it came a baseball cap, a rope belt and a small silver whistle.

Max turned the whistle over in his hands. *What's this for?* he wondered. Curiously he blew it, but no sound came out. 'Great,' he muttered. 'I always end up with stuff that's broken.'

The words were barely out of his mouth when a snort sounded from the shadows of the amphitheatre.

Max stiffened and then relaxed when a huge black horse appeared. Tentatively, he stepped towards the beast. 'Hello boy,' he said, before noticing the horse's angry red eyes. 'Uh, easy now, there's a good horsey.'

If its high-pitched whine was anything to go by, 'horsey' wasn't a name the creature appreciated. Huge feathered wings unfurled as it rose on hind legs and pawed the air. This was no horse, it was a pegasus, and it didn't look happy to see him.

Hooves thudded across the ground, sending up a dust storm. Max grabbed his uniform and ran. An impromptu game of cat and mouse followed, with Max dodging behind pillars while the pegasus pursued him with flattened ears and snapping teeth.

At the far end of the arena was a pillar that was smaller than the rest. Max thought he might be able to pull himself up on to it. He broke cover, and out of the corner of his eye saw the giant horse tear after him. He was only half way there when the pegasus bowled him over. Max flipped on to his back and at the same time the beast reared up into the air. He rolled as the creature thudded down, its hooves landing in the spot that Max's head had just occupied. Panting, Max sprang to his feet, raced to the pillar and hauled himself up. He crouched on the stone platform, clutching his uniform. *What do I do now? What do I do?*

As the pegasus thundered past, Max leapt from the pillar on to the animal's broad back. He grasped a handful of mane and bent low over the horse's neck as the animal suddenly rose into the air.

This, I was not expecting, thought Max, as he clung on for dear life.

The creature's wings beat powerfully, taking them higher and higher above the amphitheatre. Suddenly the pegasus winched in its wings and dropped like a stone. 'I'm too young to die,' whimpered Max as he left his stomach somewhere far above.

Just as they were about to become nothing but a pair of dark red splats on the arena floor, the pegasus spread its wings and soared up again, this

time performing a gravity-defying loop-the-loop. Max dug in his knees and closed his eyes. Why on earth had he thought it would be better to be *on* the beast rather than being pursued by it?

Unable to dislodge Max, the black horse landed and galloped across the arena. It suddenly halted, throwing itself back on its haunches as a huge shadow fell across the arena. Max recognised it immediately. Cerberus.

'Don't look!' He used his legs to turn the pegasus around, and at the same time leaned forward to place his robes as a blindfold over the pegasus's eyes.

As he was doing so, he caught sight of a squat figure trying to hide behind one of the pillars. 'Mopsus!' Max roared. 'Did you bring Cerberus here?'

Mopsus peeked around the pillar, his luminous eyes gleaming. In his hand he held the ornate key, the only thing Max was aware of that would pacify the monstrous three-headed guard dog.

The ground trembled as Cerberus stalked them, each footstep shaking the pillars and the arena floor. Treasure clattered on the ground behind them and the pegasus reared in fright.

'Give me the key!' Max yelled before realising that he was speaking to nothing but air.

Mopsus had disappeared.

CHAPTER EIGHT

Max dug his heels against the pegasus's sides. 'Whoa!' he shouted as the pegasus broke into a gallop from a standstill and headed straight for the opposite wall. The huge horse skidded to a halt, and Max grabbed a handful of mane to stop himself being catapulted over the creature's head. He felt a surge of temper.

'Look here, horsey,' he hissed in the pegasus's ear. 'As much as I hate to admit this, you're the only one that can get us out of here, but that's only going to happen if you engage your brain. Now why don't you try again, only this time – ' He nudged the creature's sides again. ' – go *up*!'

The pegasus flattened its ears, and for a moment Max thought it was going to refuse. He felt a gust of Cerberus's stinking hot breath on his neck and screwed his eyes shut. A moment later, a strong draught fanned away the stench. The winged horse rose into the air, and Max resisted the natural urge to look down as a triple howl of rage sounded beneath him.

'Whoop, whoop,' he yelled. He threw his arms around the pegasus's warm neck and clung on while they continued to defy gravity.

Once they had left the arena behind, Max twitched the robes off the great beast's eyes. He needn't have bothered, since a moment later they flew into darkness. All Max could do was hold on and hope for the best, until finally a huge shape appeared in the darkness front of them. It was Death's fortress.

The pegasus clattered onto a stone balcony and nosed open some double doors that led into the main hall.

Mopsus stood with his back to the fire that blazed in the hearth, warming his buttocks. His mouth dropped open at the sight of Max and the pegasus.

Max slid off the animal's back and collapsed on the ground, gasping for breath.

'Oh good.' Death looked up from where he was seated at the table. 'You've got the robes – although I had expected you to be wearing them.'

Max forced himself into a sitting position just in time for the pegasus to whip its tail against his cheek. Giving a low whinny, it trotted up to Mopsus, who fed it some of Liah's tooth-destroying bread. 'How are you, Buttercup?' he said over the sound of crunching.

'Buttercup?' Max couldn't imagine a less appropriate name. 'Killer, more like. And he's not the only one. Why did you leave me in the arena with that monster? I could have been turned to stone!'

Death slowly swivelled to face Mopsus. 'What is the boy talking about?'

'Erm, nothing really. Just a small test I devised to ensure that he's up to the task ahead of him.' Before Max could process the idea of another task, Mopsus turned to him and said sniffily, 'If you'd put on the robes before summoning Cuppy, you wouldn't have had a problem. As Death's... *assistant*,' he almost spat the word, 'any creature of the Underworld is yours to command when you're wearing them.'

'I didn't summon him,' Max objected, before remembering he had blown the silver whistle. 'Is there any other vital information you've chosen not to share with me?' He narrowed his eyes at Mopsus and flipped the baseball cap on to his head. 'What about this, for instance?'

Wordlessly Mopsus sloped across the room, collected a pewter plate from the table and held it up in front of Max.

Staring into the polished metal, Max almost passed out when nothing stared back. 'I'm invisible?' He tugged off the cap and was relieved when his reflection flickered on to the plate.

'Evidently,' Mopsus drawled. 'Do you always go out of your way to state the obvious?'

'What about the belt?' Max said faintly. 'What does that do?'

Death picked it up. '*Age quod agis.*' The belt wriggled out of his fingers and zigzagged across the floor. It slid up Max's waist and tied itself into a knot.

'So this is to save me from my jeans falling down?'

'Untie the belt and flick it at Mopsus,' Death instructed, to Mopsus's obvious annoyance.

Max did as he was told, thinking that if he *did* have a weapon it would be a pitchfork to skewer the nasty little creature.

'Interesting choice,' Mopsus sulked.

The belt had turned cold and heavy in Max's hands. Staring down, he saw it had turned into a gleaming pitchfork.

'It will turn into whatever you want, although it hasn't quite got the hang of anything automated,' Death continued. 'You are free to experiment but be warned: it has been known to get messy. Now, get dressed.'

Max yanked on the robes, which were several inches too long.

'Now you are ready,' Death told him.

'Ready for what?' Max shoved the whistle into his pocket. 'I'd have to be desperate to use that whistle again. That animal is loopy.'

Cuppy snorted, spraying Max with chunks of bread.

Death waved his bony hand, indicating Max should sit at the table. 'Mopsus is good at telling tales. He will fill you in on the background of your task.'

Mopsus sat opposite Max and waggled a finger in his ear. With a satisfied grunt he withdrew a plug of thick yellow wax and rolled it between his thumb and forefinger.

'Many centuries ago, in the city of Alexandria was a library which was famous the world over,' he said. 'Nothing has ever been built to rival it: floors of gold, pillars of silver, archways framed with diamonds and rubies. In its vaults were

61

treasures said to be gifts from the gods, including an elixir.'

Max frowned. 'You've lost me.'

'A liquid with life-giving powers,' said Mopsus, pausing to suck the wax from his fingers with obvious relish. 'The elixir could heal injuries, extend life and even bring people back from the dead. Recently something happened to make us believe that perhaps the elixir survived the library's annihilation.'

Death placed a bony hand on the table. 'Days ago a soul that was due to be harvested regenerated itself.'

'Perhaps you got the date wrong?' Max suggested. 'Or maybe there was a mix-up...' He trailed off, aware the temperature in the room had suddenly plummeted. *Another note to self, do not ever suggest that Death could make a mistake.* Max shifted uncomfortably in his chair.

Mopsus broke the silence. 'There is no error. The elixir needs to be retrieved before whoever has it can use it again. Interrupting death disrupts the natural order. If the person who has the elixir keeps using it then we're looking at a natural disaster on a grand scale. Not just for the Earth, but for the whole universe.'

Not for the first time, Max wondered why he had been chosen. The suspicion that he was being manipulated by the Grim Reaper refused to go away.

Death pushed back his chair and stalked up and down, electricity sparking from his robes.

'He is not a happy bunny,' Mopsus pointed out in a hushed tone. 'Death never usually interferes with the affairs of man. But this time, it's *personal*.'

CHAPTER NINE

'Why doesn't he just go and zap whoever it is that's got the elixir?' Max asked.

Suddenly he found himself up close and personal with Mopsus's lengthy nasal hair. 'The truth is,' Mopsus whispered, his breath almost as potent as Cerberus's, 'he's not allowed to interfere with what goes on in the Overworld. Even *he*'s accountable for his actions.'

Death rejoined them and withdrew from his cloak a leather pouch. 'Mopsus,' he boomed. 'Give the boy a key.'

Mopsus crossed the room and unhooked a familiar brass key from a hook beside the fireplace. 'Don't lose this,' he warned Max, 'it's not easy getting spare ones cut.'

Max's eyebrows shot up when he read the slogan on the machine-gun-shaped fob that was attached to the key: *I like you, so I'll kill you last*.

Death tossed over the pouch, which clinked when Max caught it. 'The address of the house is in there. Use the key to travel to the Overworld. Insert it in to any door and a pathway will open between the two worlds. It will take you to the right place.'

'You want me to find the elixir?'

Death nodded. 'Bring it to me as soon as you have it.'

Max pushed back the chair, his mouth feeling dry. He needed a drink of water before embarking on his task. His stomach growled and he figured that while he was at it he'd look for something to eat that hadn't been cooked by Liah.

He had his hand on the door when Mopsus called his name. 'We don't have to remind you not to talk about this to anyone, do we?' he said warningly.

'Uh uh,' Max said quickly, before stepping into the kitchen.

Liah had a chopping board out and was attacking something that looked as if it had spent its whole life in a dark, damp environment. She flicked a stalk on to the floor where something dark and furry pounced on it and dragged it under a kitchen unit.

Max's appetite shrivelled. 'Um, hey Liah, I'm just going to get some water.' He looked around for a tap.

'Over there.' Liah pointed to a bucket placed on a rocky sill. Water dripped into it from the ceiling.

Max set down his cap so he could scoop out a handful of the cold clear liquid.

'So, what jobs does he have lined up for you?' Liah frowned. 'And why are you wearing a pair of curtains?'

Max avoided the first question and looked down at the voluminous robes. 'Like I don't know they don't fit me. But I'm stuck with them since they're part of the job description.' He had no intention of them remaining part of the job description once he was in the Overworld. 'Do you have a bag?'

Liah put down the knife and rummaged in a kitchen cupboard. 'Here.'

Max looked at the fluffy koala bear backpack. Was she serious?

Liah shrugged. 'Mopsus likes to bring back mementos from his trips to the Overworld.' She pulled out a stool and sat down. Her green eyes coolly assessed him. 'You still haven't explained how you ended up being here.'

'I offered to play Death for my little sister's life,' Max said. 'He offered me the job instead. How about you? What happened exactly?' He remembered she had said she was down here for a similar reason.

Liah circled her finger on the table. 'My fiancé. He was in a duel – fighting someone else over me. He lost a lot of blood. Death turned up and…' Her voice wobbled. She took a deep breath. 'You know the rest.'

Max blinked. Her fiancé? She couldn't be more than a couple of years older than he was.

Liah stared past Max, clearly caught up in her memories. 'I really thought I could play him and win,' she said softly. 'When I lost, both my life and Tom's should have been taken… but Death offered me a job instead.'

'So you saved Tom's life,' Max said.

Liah sniffed. 'Yes. Just like you've saved your little sister. You must be a really good brother.'

Max suddenly wished Liah would go back to being her usual self – the girl who would sooner chew her own arm off than part with a compliment. He felt his cheeks turn hot. He wasn't a great brother to Amy.

Liah pushed back her stool, her eyes suspiciously moist. 'I need to get some beans from the stores. I'll be back in a minute.' She hurried away and Max decided now would be a good time to leave.

Tugging off his robes, he stuffed them into the backpack before heading over to the nearest door. He opened it and discovered a cupboard full of brooms and dusters. Closing the door, he inserted the key Mopsus had given him and turned it. When he opened the door again, the cleaning materials were gone. A winding staircase took their place.

Max's mood lightened with each step he took. He was leaving Death's kingdom behind, even if it was just for a few days.

At the top of the staircase was another door, which he pushed open.

Bright sunlight made his eyes water. Traffic roared, people chattered and in the distance a horn sounded. Max turned his face up to the sky to feel the warmth of the sun on his skin and took a deep gulp of fresh air.

He turned to lock the door and was surprised when it burst open, forcing him to take a step back.

Framed in the doorway was Liah.

CHAPTER TEN

'What is this place? Liah shrieked. She pointed a shaking finger at a bus rumbling past, before covering her ears with her hands and cowering against the door.

The wrong side of it, Max thought grimly. 'Liah, you have to go back!' he cried. She was acting crazy. Too much time spent in Death's kingdom clearly wasn't good for a person. He snapped his fingers in front of Liah's face, trying to get her to look at him instead of the traffic whizzing past. 'Earth to Liah? Hello? Listen to me. You need to go back. You can't stay.'

After a few minutes of trying to get Liah to focus, he gave up. He gripped her arm and towed her along the pavement to the nearest café.

He pushed Liah into a chair. 'What is wrong with you? It's like you've never...' He broke off when a dark-haired man with olive skin approached them.

'What can I get you?' the man asked in a heavy accent.

Max ordered the first thing he saw on the menu and turned his attention back to Liah. He finally had an inkling of what might be wrong. 'Liah, what year was it when you went down into the Underworld?'

There was a long silence. '1842,' said Liah, at last. She took a deep breath. 'How long have I been down there, Max?'

Max did some quick calculations in his head. 'About a hundred and seventy years.'

Liah eyes brimmed with tears. 'He'll be dead,' she whispered. 'All this time he's been in the Underworld, while I've been working in Death's kitchen.'

Max realised she was talking about Tom. He tried to think of something positive to say. 'At least when you go back you'll be able to find him.'

Liah blinked rapidly, her expression suddenly becoming like flint. 'I'm not allowed to mix with the dead.'

'Well,' said Max, racking his brains for anything that might sound helpful, 'at least you can move on now. Find someone else?'

Liah's eyebrows shot up.

'Listen, I'm not on a short-term contract like you. I'm in the Underworld for the duration. And FYI, I'm not ready to "move on". It doesn't feel like a hundred and seventy years since I was last with Tom! It feels like we've been apart for months, not over a century…' Her voice wobbled.

At that moment their food arrived. Max finished his margherita pizza in record time before eyeing Liah's. She'd only nibbled at one piece so far.

'You don't sound like you're from Victorian England,' he commented, thinking that changing the subject from dead boyfriends could only be a good thing.

Liah shrugged. 'Mopsus often comes in to chat while I'm working; he's not so bad once you get used to him. He's always spying on what's going on up here. He picks up the lingo and I suppose some of it must rub off on me.' She paused. 'Where do you think we are?'

'I think we may be on one of the Greek Islands,' Max replied, jabbing a finger at the café's address on the menu. 'Heraklion. I'm pretty sure that's in Crete.' He pushed back his chair. 'Come on. We need to get you back before Death finds out you're missing.'

Liah stared up at him. 'I'm not going back. I'm staying with you.'

'You can't.' Max was firm. 'I'm on a job and I'm supposed to be doing it *alone*.'

Liah folded her arms. 'I'm not about to let you try and find the elixir all on your own. If you fail and the universe implodes I won't get another chance to come above ground, and Death owes me a hundred and seventy years' worth of holiday leave.'

Max sank back down into his chair. 'You know about the elixir?'

'Of course.' Liah waved her hand dismissively. 'The only thing that stops me going insane from boredom is being able to listen to what goes on in Death's private quarters.'

They were interrupted by a waiter coming to clear their table.

Max discovered some money in the pouch Death had given him, and handed over several coins.

'What kind of money is this?' The waiter turned one of the tarnished gold coins back and forth, looking confused.

Max's heart sank. Whatever he had handed over certainly wasn't euros, and he didn't have any other money on him. 'Uh...' He hesitated before suddenly bolting towards the door. 'Run!' he yelled to a startled Liah.

He darted down a nearby alleyway and ducked into a doorway. He thought of his baseball cap and how useful it would be right now, but stupidly he must have left it behind in Death's kitchen.

Minutes later, Liah strolled up. 'I don't know why you're hiding,' she said calmly. 'Those coins you've just paid him are enough to buy his entire café, never mind a couple of pizzas.'

Max felt his cheeks turn red. He fumbled in the pouch and withdrew the address Death had given him. 'We'll get a taxi. You know, pay someone to take us to the address.'

Liah shrugged. 'Whatever. Just make sure that this time you get change.'

* * *

The house was a ten-minute drive from the town. Set on a hill in a secluded position, it had far-reaching sea views and was surrounded by sprawling grounds full of olive trees.

'Whoever lives here has money,' Max commented, staring up at the red-roofed two-storey building.

Liah nodded. 'Lots of it.'

She had been subdued during the car journey as she'd brooded over the previous hour's revelations, but when they arrived at the house she had set off up the drive looking determined. Max had trailed a few feet behind, trying to work out who exactly it was that had been given the role of Death's assistant.

'You need to see if anyone's in,' Liah told him.

'Brilliant,' Max said sarcastically. 'Why didn't I think of that?'

'And if they're not,' Liah continued as if he hadn't spoken, 'you'll be able to break in and find the elixir.' Her gaze slid away from the house and she stared up at the sky, a frown denting her brow. Before Max had a chance to see what it was she was looking at, she shrieked and ran toward the nearest tree. Throwing herself down on the ground she tucked up into a ball, her head covered by her arms.

'What's the matter now?' Max called, feeling exasperated.

A moment later a plane screamed overhead, making Liah screech in terror.

Max's lips twitched. He went to join her, crouching down as he said reassuringly, 'It's a plane. I forgot to tell you about them. People travel in them – like cars.'

Liah peeped through her hands. 'But it was flying. How could it stay up in the air?'

'That's a very good question,' Max said. He didn't want to admit that he didn't really have a clue. 'It's all to do with balancing the ratio of velocity with the shape of the wings,' he hazarded.

Liah frowned as she mouthed what he had just said.

Wanting to avoid any more questions, Max strode toward the house. 'I'll knock on the door,' he said when Liah caught up with him. 'If anyone answers we'll pretend that we've got the wrong address.'

They climbed the steps to the veranda and Max pressed the doorbell. Nervously, they waited.

The house remained silent.

'I can't see anything through this stuff.' Liah pressed her nose against the frosted glass door.

They walked around the veranda and spotted a small window that had been left open. Max managed to get his head and one arm through the cramped space but when it came to fitting his other arm through the gap, he struggled.

'Twist,' Liah advised. She took hold of his feet and pushed hard.

'Stop shoving,' Max yelped, feeling the window frame bite into his chest.

'I don't know what you're making such a fuss about,' Liah retorted. 'If you can get your head through then the rest of your body should follow.'

Max finally dragged his second arm through the gap, and was now dangling half in and half out of the house. 'Go around to the front door and I'll let you in,' he panted.

Liah had only been gone a moment when he heard a soft click. He strained his ears to hear. A second click followed the first.

It was the front door closing.

Max frantically wriggled, but his belt caught on the latch and he couldn't move in either direction. Stranded, he raised his head as the owner of the house walked into the living room.

The man dropped the bag he was carrying and looked across at Max.

Max couldn't believe what he was seeing.

For what felt like ages they stared at each other. Finally Max spoke.

'Hello, Dad.'

CHAPTER ELEVEN

'Max?' Dropping his shopping bags, Max's father strode across the room. He reached up, grasped Max under the arms and pulled him through the window.

Max's mind raced. This was his dad's house? Suddenly pieces of the jigsaw puzzle seemed to slot together. So *this* was why he'd been selected as Death's assistant. Because he'd be able to get close to the person who had the elixir. His eyes flickered nervously to the opposite door. He wondered if Liah would have the sense to stay out of sight. It was going to be hard enough to explain his own presence, never mind hers.

'What are you doing here?' Max's father asked.

'I … er … wanted to find you. It's not unusual is it, for someone to want to know where their dad is?' Max looked past his father. Having walked in through the unlocked front door, Liah stood in the living room doorway. She didn't look at all surprised by the revelation that they were in his father's house.

'How did you find me?'

Max was speechless. He couldn't come up with a plausible explanation for how he tracked down his father. It wasn't like he could tell the truth – *a seven-foot skeleton gave me the address*. 'I… um… could I have a glass of water?' Making his voice sound weak wasn't difficult. 'I'm not feeling good.'

'Of course! Go and sit down and I'll bring it to you,' his dad said. He turned around and caught sight of Liah.

'Hi,' Liah smiled. She smoothed out the wrinkles on her distinctly cobwebby black dress. 'I'm Liah. I'm Max's… friend. He can't go anywhere without me.' She lowered her voice. 'He has phobias,' she whispered conspiratorially, 'and severe abandonment issues.'

'What a joker,' Max countered hurriedly, looking daggers at Liah. 'Always making up funny stories!'

Max's father threw a confused glance over his shoulder before moving into the kitchen to fill a glass with water.

'Get a grip,' Liah hissed, dragging Max over to the sofa. 'You're going to blow this big time if you carry on acting so weird.'

Max scowled at her. 'Because of course, you're always totally in control,' he said sarcastically.

Liah's cheeks flushed. 'Whatever.'

Max rubbed his fingers against his temples. He couldn't believe he was in his dad's house. *What's he been doing all this time? Why's he never been in touch?* He forced himself to smile as his father headed over carrying a tray.

Max tried to focus on explaining away his sudden appearance. 'Things aren't great at home,' he said, deciding to stick as closely to the truth as possible. 'I needed to get away for a while so I came here. I thought we could spend Christmas together.'

'The three of us?' Max's dad glanced worriedly at Liah, who gave him an encouraging smile. 'Uh, there's something moving in your hair,' he told her.

Liah reached up and plucked a spider out of her hair. She casually flicked it away and it scuttled under the sofa.

'Was that a black widow?' said Max's dad, his voice rising an octave. He shook his head, as if to somehow convince himself that any second

everything would start making sense, and turned
his attention back to Max. 'Where have you come
from? You're still living in Wales, aren't you?
Did you get on a plane all by yourself? Or rather,
with your, er... girlfriend? How did you get my
address?'

Max jumped in with some answers, concerned
his father was going to go into meltdown. 'I live
in Scotland now, with Mum. You know she got
re-married, right, and had a baby? Not that she's
a baby any more.' He hurried on, afraid that if he
dwelt on the subject of Amy he'd follow his father

into meltdown territory. 'Liah's just a... um... friend. She's looking for a job out here.'

'Holiday job,' Liah said when Max's father's frown deepened. 'Waitressing. I've done a lot of that sort of thing before, er, sir.'

'Call me Greg.' Max's dad returned his attention to Max and asked the question he was dreading.

'Does your mother know you're here?'

* * *

Max perched on the edge of the sofa. He'd promised to call his mother immediately and while part of him was longing to hear her voice, the other part was dreading the tongue lashing he was no doubt about to receive. With a sigh he finally picked up the receiver.

As soon as Max's mother heard his voice she burst into tears. 'Where are you? We've been worried sick! Where have you been? Are you alright?'

'I'm fine,' he said quickly. 'I'm really sorry, Mum. I didn't want you to worry.'

'What do you mean you didn't want me to worry?' Her voice rose. 'What did you think I'd do when you disappeared for *two whole days*?'

So that was how much time had passed in the Overworld since he'd been away. Max swallowed. 'I didn't think. I've been really selfish and I'm *really* sorry.'

'Where are you?' she asked again.

'I'm at... Dad's.' He tensed, waiting for an explosion on the other end of the line.

Instead his announcement was met with a long silence; so long, in fact, that Max began to wonder if his mother had hung up. 'Where?' she finally whispered.

'Crete.'

'Crete?' She seemed unable to speak in words longer than one syllable.

Before Max could say anything else the phone was taken out of his hand. Greg winked reassuringly at him before speaking into the handset. He listened while his father offered to have him over Christmas before handing back the phone.

'I can't pretend to understand why you're doing this,' his mother said bitterly. 'As if we haven't had enough worry over Amy.'

'Is she okay?'

'She's fine now. She's asking for you. She's convinced that a bogeyman's taken you away.' She took a shuddering breath. 'We'd looked forward to a family Christmas together, and it feels as if you've torn that up into little bits and thrown it back in our faces.'

'Mum...' Max didn't know what to say.

'I can't talk to you any more right now,' she sniffed. 'I'm just too upset. Call me again tomorrow, OK?'

'OK.'

After he hung up Max lay back on the sofa and stared up at the ceiling until his eyes ached. How was he ever going to make this up to his mother?

* * *

That evening Max laid the table while his dad fried fish, serving it up with golden chips.

'Come on,' Max called over to Liah who was sitting cross-legged on the sofa staring in awe at Greg's laptop screen.

'You've got to see this!' she cried. 'If I click the rat, music plays!'

Max crossed the room. 'I've already told you, it's called a mouse,' he murmured. 'Come on, it's time to eat.'

Greg forked up flakes of soft white fish. 'You're welcome to stay here with us if you've not got anywhere else to go,' he told Liah.

Liah shot Max a surprised look. 'How long is Max staying, Greg?' she asked pointedly.

Max suddenly developed an intense interest in making sure all of the bones had been removed from his fish.

'Oh, you know, a week, maybe two,' replied Greg happily.

'Right.' Liah had the ability to make single syllables ooze significance.

Max finally looked back up to meet her accusing stare.

'Thanks very much for the kind offer,' she told Greg without breaking eye contact with Max. 'But I won't be staying longer than a night, two at the most.'

Greg shrugged, seemingly oblivious to the tense atmosphere. Over dessert he chatted briefly about his job. 'I'm a location scout. I travel around the world finding the best places for films to be shot in.'

Max felt a rush of pride. His dad was so cool.

'What's a film?' asked Liah, sweetly.

Max spent the evening playing chess with Greg

while Liah returned with rapt attention to the laptop.

'Why did you leave?' The question had left Max's lips before he'd even consciously thought of asking it.

Greg sighed. 'It was complicated. I always meant to come back, you know. But by the time I was ready, your mother had moved on.'

I knew it! thought Max. His dad had always meant to return. If his mother hadn't married David, his dad would have come back and they would have been a family once again.

'I always suspected you'd come and find me, that you'd strike out and do what you wanted.' He reached out to ruffle Max's hair. 'You're a chip off the old block.'

* * *

Later that night, Liah walked into Max's bedroom. She perched on the end of the bed and glared at him. 'We can't stay with your dad for Christmas. We've got a job to do, and we've got to do it, *now*.'

'No, *I've* got a job to do,' Max pointed out. 'And it's up to me how I do it.'

'You *know* that all you're supposed to be doing is looking for the elixir,' Liah hissed. 'This isn't the time to be playing happy families.'

Max sat up. 'Talking of knowing things. You knew this was my dad's house before we even came to the Overworld, didn't you?'

Liah became engrossed in examining her fingernails. 'I might have heard something,' she said.

'Yeah, right,' Max said. 'You knew and you didn't warn me!'

In the following silence a picture fell off the wall, landing with a clatter on the floor.

'That's the second time today,' Liah frowned. 'Earlier a magazine fell off the coffee table even though I wasn't anywhere near it.'

Max shrugged. He had enough on his mind without worrying about possible poltergeist activity. 'Trust me, I know what I'm doing. Although I don't think for one minute that my dad's got anything to do with the elixir.' After spending some time with his father, Max was convinced that there had to be someone else involved.

Liah folded her arms. 'Well, that's what we're here to find out. And fast.'

CHAPTER TWELVE

The following night Max suddenly awoke. He wondered what had disturbed him as he yawned and went to stretch, and then realised he couldn't move his legs. He struggled against the dead weight crushing them, before thrashing out in an attempt to switch on the bedside light.

Two pinpricks of amber glowed in the dark. 'No need for the light,' growled a familiar voice. An equally familiar stink wafted across the room.

Max's fingers plucked nervously against the sheets. He hadn't had a chance to look for the elixir, because his dad had taken them out for the day sightseeing.

Not that it matters, he thought. *Dad doesn't have it. There's no way he'd be involved with this kind of supernatural weirdness.* He went on the defensive. 'I haven't found the elixir, and if you ask me I don't think it's here.'

'Interesting.' Mopsus adjusted his position so that he weighed even more heavily on Max's legs. Max bit his lip to stop himself from crying out. 'I'm curious to know on what you are basing your opinion. How hard have you actually tried to find it?'

Silence stretched between them, before the weight finally lifted from Max's legs and light flooded the room. Max shouted out as Mopsus's warty face suddenly appeared nose to nose with his.

Mopsus clamped a gnarled hand over Max's mouth and said, 'So, can I inform Death that you intend to look for the elixir right away? You do remember what's at stake if you fail to deliver?'

Max felt as if he'd had a bucket of cold water sloshed over him. *Amy.* As soon as the stinking creature withdrew his hand, Max said, 'I'll search the house tonight.'

'Fantastic.' Mopsus broke into a grin, and a few maggots made a desperate bid for freedom from between his rotten teeth. 'Don't forget to wear your robes. Oh, and tell Liah I'm covering for her in the kitchen.' Mopsus rubbed his stomach. 'The food's never been so good.'

Before Max could reply Mopsus vanished.

'Tonight,' Max spoke aloud. A shiver ran down his spine as he flicked a maggot off his bed.

He wasn't ready.

* * *

Max waited for the house to be silent before creeping from his room, feeling like an idiot clad in his orange robes. Moonlight illuminated the living room, which he carefully searched. He rifled through the shelves and drawers without finding anything even remotely suspect.

Quietly he padded along to his dad's study. Unlike the rest of the house, it was full of furniture and every surface was littered with papers. Shelves lining the walls overflowed with books and files. Max hesitated. *Where do I begin?* He'd be here all night hunting for something he was sure wouldn't be found. He knelt down and began to search through a pile of cardboard boxes stacked beside the desk.

As he rifled through paperwork he heard a soft click. He whipped around to look at the door, rapidly trying to think up a reason for being in his dad's study so late at night.

No one was there.

Max crept over to the door, opened it and looked up and down the hallway. No one was there either.

He slipped back into the study and double-checked that the door was properly shut. Once he had finished searching through the boxes, he moved on to his dad's desk. Carefully he slid out the middle drawer, and yelled.

Someone had grabbed his leg.

He staggered back and fell, hitting the floor with a spine-jarring bump.

A pair of piercing green eyes met his angry gaze. Liah was crouched in the small alcove under the desk. 'What are you doing here?' Max snapped.

'What you should have been doing since we got here,' she snapped. 'Looking for the elixir.'

'Have you found it?'

'I'd only just started looking when you came in. I didn't know it was you so I hid under here...' She broke off at the sound of voices just outside the door.

Max felt a fresh wave of panic. 'Move up,' he hissed.

'There's no room. Find somewhere else!'

Max shoved her and tried to force his way under the desk.

'You'll get us both caught.' She pinched his arm.

Max saw the door handle turning. Frantically he looked for somewhere else to hide. Hanging over the glass doors that led on to the veranda were long curtains. As the door swung open, Max shot behind them. He froze, trying not to breathe. His heart hammered against his chest.

He heard his father speak. 'The drop off's at midnight – that only leaves us twenty minutes to get there.'

'You haven't left us with a lot of time,' another male voice replied.

'I've got unexpected houseguests,' came Greg's terse response. 'I had to wait until they were asleep.'

The hairs on the back of Max's neck prickled. What were they going to drop off that was so secret? Could his dad really have the elixir? Liah would be unbearable if she was proven right.

A loud crash made him jump.

'What was that?' Greg's companion exclaimed.

'Relax, it was just some books falling down,' said Greg.

'Books don't just jump off shelves of their own accord.'

'You can see there's no one there, Ralf.' Greg sounded impatient.

'Have you checked the doors are locked?'

Max peered around the curtain and saw a well-built, blond-haired man stride towards him. Max's mouth turned dry. He thought longingly of his invisibility cap. How was he going to explain what he was doing here?

Ralf's hand grasped the edge of the curtain just as a loud, fake-sounding sneeze broke the silence.

'Who's there?' Greg demanded.

Without pulling back the curtain, Ralf strode away.

Max peered into the room again in time to see his father reach down and pull Liah out from under the desk. 'Liah! What are you doing here?'

Liah stared at the two men defiantly. She pressed her lips together and refused to say anything.

'We haven't time for this,' Ralf said. 'What are we going to do with her?'

Greg thrust Liah at him before taking a key out of his pocket. He used it to unlock a slim drawer in the centre of his desk. Carefully he withdrew a small silver casket. 'Bring her with us,' he said grimly. 'We're not letting her go until she tells us what exactly she's doing here.'

CHAPTER THIRTEEN

This was bad, seriously bad. Max listened to the distant sound of tyres squealing. What was he going to do? Where had they gone? He had to find them. Liah had done what she could to save him, now it was his turn to return the favour.

He fumbled in his pocket and pulled out the silver whistle, which he'd hoped not to have to use. He blew through it desperately, praying that its soundless note would summon Buttercup as quickly in the Overworld.

At once, a clatter of hooves sounded outside. Max pulled back the door and found the huge pegasus waiting. He snorted and pawed the ground when Max drew close.

'Stop with the big man routine,' Max said irritably. 'It doesn't fool anyone. Not with a name like Buttercup.' He grasped a handful of mane and scrambled onto the pegasus's back. 'You like

Liah, don't you? Even if she does bake bread hard enough to break teeth. You need to help me get her back.' He then spoke the words he'd always wanted to say. 'Follow that car. Go!'

Cuppy rose in the air, his wings beating powerfully.

Max's stomach flipped as the black horse soared after the car. The wind whistled in his ears as they followed the vehicle along winding mountain roads to a white villa perched on a hilltop. Its high spiked fence and gate presented no challenge to the pegasus, which soared over them before easily landing behind a huge bush.

Max slid off, and stumbled forward when Cuppy nudged him in the back. 'I'm going, I'm going,' he muttered. He parted the thick branches of the bush and peered through a gap in the foliage. Up ahead his dad, Ralf and Liah disappeared through the villa's double doors. Max scurried across the broad expanse of lawn and climbed the steps leading to the entrance. Before he could reach the door it slowly opened. Max froze, knowing he had nowhere to hide from whoever was about to come out.

Seconds ticked by but no one appeared, so Max crept over to the entrance. Through the open door he spotted the men and Liah heading down a long hallway. After a quick check to make sure there was no one else around, Max slipped inside and silently closed the door behind him.

As he hurried along the dark passageway, he almost caught up with the small group of shadowy figures ahead, before realising that he had no idea how he'd make them release Liah. They stopped suddenly and Max froze, pressing himself against the wall, hoping the moonlight wouldn't pick him out. A key turned in a lock and two figures moved away, their footsteps growing faint.

Liah! She must be behind that door. Having learned from his zombie experience, Max assessed the situation coolly. Luckily for him, they'd left the key in the lock. *Another door thwarted*, thought Max.

Liah was pacing the room, her hands tied behind her back, her mouth covered in tape. 'Mmmmh, mumphh,' she muttered.

Max reached out and yanked off the tape.

'Ouch!' she complained. 'Watch it.' She turned around so he could untie her hands.

'Thanks,' he said awkwardly. 'For covering for me.' He waited for her sarcastic response and was surprised when all she did was shrug.

'Come on,' Liah said. 'We've got to get that elixir.'

They hurried along the passage and a short way along they stopped and gripped each other. One of the flagstones on the floor was moving all on its own. Slowly it slid back revealing a cavity below.

'How did that happen?' Liah hissed, her fingers tightening on Max's arm.

Max pointed to a small lever on the opposite wall. 'I bet that's what opened it. Chill, Liah. The place for ghosts is in the Underworld, not here.' Ignoring the voice in his head that questioned just who had pressed the lever, he edged forward. He peered into the opening and saw a narrow flight of stone steps leading to a dimly lit passage. 'Come on. Follow me.'

He dropped through the hole and took the steps two at a time. Before he reached the bottom his feet slid out from underneath him. 'Oomph!' He bumped down the remaining steps and collided with something at the bottom.

'Are you alright?' Liah reached down and pulled him up. Suddenly her grip went slack and Max bumped back down again.

'Wha–' Max looked up indignantly.

Liah stared past him to the foot of the stairs. Her face was even paler than usual. She looked as if she had seen a ghost.

Max followed her stare to where a young man wearing decidedly old-fashioned clothes was straightening up. He held in his hands a modern baseball cap – a familiar-looking baseball cap. 'Hey, that's mine!' Max said. 'How did you get that?' He was positive he'd left it in Death's kitchen.

There was something seriously weird going on with the guy's appearance. He shimmered and flickered like a hologram as he went to put the baseball cap back on his head.

Max shot forward. 'Oh no you don't!' He snatched it away before the person could vanish. 'How long have you had this?'

The young man ignored him. He was looking at Liah.

'Who are you?' Max felt as if the ground could swallow him up right now and neither of them would notice. 'What's going on?'

'It's Tom,' Liah finally whispered. 'He's Tom.'

The young man's expression flickered into a smile. 'Hello, Liah,' he said. 'Have you missed me?'

Max disliked Tom on the spot. Maybe it was because of the way Tom was blanking him, although it could have had something to do with the way Tom towered over him. It could also have something to do with the way that Liah was gazing at Tom as if he were some kind of god. It *definitely* had something to do with the fact that Tom had stolen Max's hat.

Max snapped his fingers in front of Liah's face. 'Earth to Liah! Weren't you the one telling me we had to get the elixir? Something about the universe imploding?'

Liah ignored him. 'You're a ghost,' she said hoarsely. 'When did you…'

'Die?' Tom said cheerfully. 'Two years after you disappeared. What happened? One moment I'm heading towards a bright light after duelling in your honour, the next I'm seeing you disappear with a giant walking, talking skeleton and I'm fine!'

'You only lived for two more years after I left?' Liah gasped. 'That's all?'

Tom shrugged. 'Oh, you know, all those nineteenth-century duels could play havoc with a fellow's health.'

'Right, I'll just leave the two of you to your cosy chat and I'll try to find the elixir on my own.'

Max thrust the cap into his pocket and pushed past Tom.

'Whoa, not so fast,' Tom said. 'We'll come with you.'

Max narrowed his eyes. Why would Tom want to help? And just what was he doing here anyway? He added suspicion to dislike. 'Aren't you supposed to ask, "What elixir?" I don't suppose you know anything about a recent spate of falling objects or magically self-opening and -closing doors?'

Tom grinned and held out his hand to Liah. 'Come on!'

Liah reached out but her hand passed straight through his. 'I can't touch you,' she sighed. 'Only the assistant's robes give the wearer the power to touch the dead. How is it that you're here, Tom? Have you been with us ever since we left the Underworld?'

In Max's opinion, Tom suddenly looked shifty – like he'd been caught with his fingers in the till.

'Do you mind if we walk and talk?' Max said pointedly. He didn't know how far ahead his father was with the elixir. *I have to get it. If I don't, Death will sack me and then it will be all over for Amy. And I'll end up like Tom.* He strode along the passageway, aware of Tom and Liah trailing behind.

'There are rumours all over the Underworld that the elixir can give back life. Is it true?' Tom asked.

'Yes,' Liah told him. 'We have to get it back before it's used again.'

Tom was silent for a moment and then said, 'The Grim Reaper wouldn't miss a drop or two would he?'

Max waited for Liah to shoot Tom down in flames.

'I guess one or two drops wouldn't do any harm,' she said slowly.

Max spun around. 'What? Only a couple of days ago you were talking about the end of the world happening if we didn't get the elixir back.'

Liah glared at him. 'I've given more than a lifetime of service to Death, and all the while Tom's been dead. The least he can do is give us back our time together.'

Behind Liah's back Tom grinned and raised an eyebrow.

Before Max could punch him, a gunshot rang out, echoing down the passage. Max turned around and raced towards the sound. *Please let Dad be okay!*

Up ahead was a narrow spiral stairway set into a wall. Max hurried up the twisting flight feeling giddy and breathless. Liah and Tom followed close behind, although only Liah's footsteps could be heard clattering against the stone steps.

Light flooded out from a room at the top of the staircase. Max would have dashed in but felt a tug on the back of his robes. 'Don't be an idiot, you can't just burst in there,' Liah hissed.

'Okay, okay, you can let me go now,' Max panted, realising Liah had just saved him from making a stupid mistake. He reached into his pocket and pulled out his cap. Putting it on he stepped into the room.

It appeared to be some kind of laboratory. It didn't have bubbling test tubes but everything was either metallic or tiled. Crowded around a stainless steel table were his father, Ralf and another man.

Max's hand flew up to cover his mouth as he realised what they were staring at. Lying on its side was a mongrel dog, its long shaggy coat sticky with blood. It wasn't moving.

Max watched his dad take a tiny glass bottle out of the silver casket. He very gently unscrewed the stopper and carefully placed a drop on to the dog's wound.

All eyes fixed on the dog.

The silence was broken by a whimper.

It works, Max thought. *The elixir really does work.* The dog lifted its head and feebly wagged its tail. *How did my dad get hold of it?*

Ralf pushed a gun back in to his jacket pocket. 'Is that evidence enough, Mr Hoffman?' he asked.

The balding man looked up and smiled slowly. 'Call me Larry.'

CHAPTER FOURTEEN

Overhead an ominous rumble sounded. Every eye swivelled up to the ceiling.

'What was that?' Greg frowned.

Max knew exactly what it was. It was thunder – the kind of thunderclap you read about when the gods have been angered.

'Let's wrap this thing up,' Larry said briskly.

'Have you got the money?' Ralf asked.

Larry gave a short dry laugh. 'You think I would just hand over a hundred million euros without seeing with my own eyes that this stuff actually works?'

'You'll make that amount a hundred times over once you've found out how to replicate the elixir,' Greg pointed out.

Ralf's expression darkened. 'I think you've been wasting our time...'

'Relax,' Larry interrupted. 'The money's here, but it's in a safe. There's a million in cash and the rest will be made by electronic transfer.' He jerked his head at a door at the opposite end of the room. 'This way.'

A hundred million euros! Max was having a hard time getting his head around such a huge sum of money.

Ralph followed Larry through into the adjoining room, shutting the door firmly behind them.

'Max, you've got to stop them,' Liah hissed.

Max was already untying his belt. What were the words Death had spoken to make the belt turn into a weapon? 'How's your haggis?' he attempted.

Nothing happened.

'Cage your maggots,' he tried again.

'Oh for goodness sake, it's *Age quod agis*,' Liah snapped.

Greg looked their way, his eyes wide with surprise.

'*Age quod agis*,' Max gabbled, imagining the first weapon that came to mind. The rope turned into a long length of braided leather. *What, so I'm Indiana Jones now?* He stepped forwards. 'Give me that,' he said to his father. His voice came out as a squeak, nothing like the butt-kicking tone he'd been going for.

106

Greg's mouth opened in terror. Max suddenly realised that he and the bullwhip were still invisible.

He pulled off his hat and watched Greg's terror turn to shock.

'Give me the elixir, Dad.' Max twitched the whip warningly.

'Max…' His dad looked nervously at the closed door behind him. 'I have no idea how you got here or what's going on but you need to get out of here, now. This is none of your business.'

Max wondered how he could possibly get his dad to part with the elixir. What could be worth more than a hundred million euros? Suddenly he knew. 'It's Amy,' he said. 'I need the elixir to save her.'

Greg looked confused. 'Is she sick? Your mum didn't mention – '

'She'll die without the elixir,' Max burst out. 'I have to have it, Dad.'

'I'm sorry, Max,' Greg held out his hands in apology. 'When I've got the money I'll give you some of it to help her. But you have to understand, bad things happen in life. What makes you a man is learning to deal with them.'

He's really ready to let Amy die so he can get his stinking, lousy money, Max realised. Never had he felt such rage – not even on the day when his dad had walked out on them. Realisation hit him like a freight train. *David would have turned down the money in an instant if it meant saving me.*

Gritting his teeth, Max leapt forwards and snatched the elixir.

'Thank you, Max.' Liah plucked the tiny bottle out of his hand.

'W-w-w-hat's going on?' Max's dad whispered, looking from Max, to Liah, to Tom. 'Is that a … that can't be a … is that a ghost?'

Max spun around. 'You've got to be joking,' he shouted at Liah, then to his father he added, 'Of course it's a ghost!'

'Boo,' interjected Tom, grinning.

Max's father suddenly looked extremely pale. 'I don't feel well,' he muttered, and slumped to the floor in a faint.

'Dad!' cried Max.

'Leave him,' said Liah. 'We've got to get out of here.'

'I'm not leaving him.' Max tried to lift his dad from under the arms. 'Help me!'

'OK,' hissed Liah, grabbing one of Greg's legs with her free hand, 'but keep the noise down or they'll hear you.'

'You can't really think the two of you are going to be together again?' Max muttered as they painstakingly dragged his father towards the stairs.

Tom nodded. 'Of course. Liah's the love of my life. Once I've had the elixir we'll be together forever.'

'Until you die,' Max pointed out. 'And considering it's Death you're cheating, I wouldn't count on being left alone to live happily ever after.'

Liah glanced uncertainly from Max to Tom.

'Just one or two drops, Liah,' encouraged Tom, 'that's all I need, and then it will be like the old days.'

'Not quite,' Max said, wondering how they were going to get his dad down the stairs. 'For a start, nobody's allowed to fight duels anymore.'

'That's not a bad idea,' Tom grinned, 'since I nearly died when I fought over Liah.'

'What was the name of the girl you actually died for?' Max said, as innocently as he could.

'Sarah,' replied Tom.

CHAPTER FIFTEEN

The silence that followed was even thicker than one of Liah's stews.

'Sarah?' Liah finally whispered. 'I thought *I* was the love of your life?'

'You are,' Tom said hastily. 'Sarah didn't mean a thing compared to you.'

'Well, she was worth dying for,' Max pointed out, laying down his dad at the top of the stairs.

'While I was slogging in the kitchen so you could be saved,' Liah hissed.

'But I was willing to die for you first!' Tom said plaintively.

Max made a swooping action with one of his hands. 'You have crashed and burned, my friend.'

'And,' Liah added furiously, 'I note that you've never once looked me up in the Underworld.' She turned to Max. 'Get him away from me – now!'

Max was happy to help. He seized Tom's arm and dragged him over to the balcony doors. Inserting Death's key into the lock, he opened the doors. Instead of the welcoming glow of the night sky, he saw a familiar staircase lit with an ominous red glow. Tom began to struggle, determined not to return to the Underworld, but his ghostly strength was no match for a living human.

'You know what they say,' Max panted as he shoved Tom through the doorway. 'Hell has no fury like a woman scorned.'

He banged the door shut and turned the key again before turning back to Liah and his unconscious father. Two bright spots of colour burned on her pale cheeks. 'Are you okay?'

Liah nodded and tilted her chin. 'Never better.'

At that moment, a catch clicked and Ralf and Larry pushed open the doors at the far end of the room.

'What the hell!' roared Ralf, pulling the gun from his pocket.

'Watch out!' Max cried as the man aimed at Liah and began to close in on her.

'Ow, my head,' muttered Max's dad, dragging himself to his feet by the stairwell. 'What's happening? Ralf?'

Liah held up the elixir. 'Come any closer and I'll smash it,' she warned.

Ralf laughed unpleasantly. 'Do that and you won't have anything left to bargain with.'

Liah narrowed her green eyes. 'I'm done with striking bargains.' She opened her fingers and let go of the glass bottle.

'No!' Greg, Larry and Ralf shouted in unison as the glass tumbled through the air and smashed into tiny shards on the floor.

'You little…' Whatever bad name Ralf called Liah was drowned by the sound of a gunshot.

Liah looked down and then back at Max. She frowned slightly as a scarlet stain spread over her chest. 'I don't feel very well,' she said.

Max got to her just as she hit the floor.

'What were you thinking! She's just a kid, Ralf!' Max's dad yelled.

Max heard the sound of running feet, followed by his father's fist connecting hard with Ralf's face, but all he could focus on was Liah. Frantically he dipped the corner of his robe into the rapidly evaporating elixir and squeezed out a drop on to Liah's wound. 'Come on, come on,' he muttered. 'Heal.'

When nothing happened he shouted again, 'Heal, will you!' He felt tears burning his eyes. Liah couldn't be dead – she'd had never really had a chance to live.

'Steady,' Liah muttered without opening her eyes. 'I'm beginning to think you care.'

Max hunkered back on his heels and let out his breath. 'You're okay.' He helped her up as another rumble of thunder sounded overhead.

Ralf staggered past them, his hands cupped over his bloody nose. He stumbled against the wall and slowly slid to the floor.

Max spun around in time to see his dad wrestle a briefcase away from Larry and swing it at his head. Larry's eyes rolled up and his knees buckled. Before he'd hit the deck, Max's dad had sprinted out of the room.

'Oh no you don't,' Max muttered as his father's footsteps rang out down the spiral staircase. 'You're not running out on me for a second time without saying goodbye.' He pulled the whistle out of his pocket and blew into it.

Lightning flashed outside the balcony windows, illuminating the outline of a rearing winged horse. Seconds later its hooves thudded down on the balcony doors, the glass shattering from their frames as they burst open. Buttercup trotted into the room and pawed the ground dramatically. 'How do you always get here so fast?' Max wondered out loud, before grabbing a handful of mane and pulling himself up.

'Don't go without me.' Liah put her foot on top of Max's and used it to scramble up behind him.

Max leaned forward, trying to ignore Liah's fingers digging into him. 'There's a bad man I need you to find, Cuppy,' he said. 'I don't want you to hurt him but I don't mind if you want to play with him a bit.'

The pegasus pawed the ground again before turning and launching itself off the balcony.

'Hang on!' Max shouted to Liah as Buttercup swooped from the tower.

'What are you going to say to him when we catch him?' Liah shouted in his ear.

Max didn't know. 'I guess I'll find out when it happens.'

CHAPTER SIXTEEN

Cuppy circled the house until Max's dad burst out of the main entrance and ran towards the car, his speed hampered by the heaviness of the case he was carrying.

Galloping through the air, the great horse's hooves were noiseless as he bore down on the desperate figure. As soon as Cuppy drew close enough, he dropped out of the sky like a stone. Baring his teeth, he grasped Greg's jacket, pulled him from the ground and started shaking him from side to side like a rag doll. The briefcase flew from his hands and hit a tree. Bursting open on impact, wads of notes spilled all over the ground. 'My money!' screamed Greg.

Max shook his head in disbelief. His dad had just been picked up and shaken around by a flying horse and all he could think about was money?

'Put him down, Cuppy!' Max ordered.

116

The black horse just snorted and continued to shake his prey.

'Now!' Max shouted.

The pegasus dropped Greg and then made what Max felt sure was a deliberately bumpy landing. He slid off and stared down at his dad who was sitting holding his head. 'Why did you leave me and Mum?' Max asked. 'And for once, would you give me a straight answer?'

'Yeah,' Liah agreed, 'or we'll set our pegasus on you.'

'A straight answer,' his dad groaned. 'That's ironic coming from the two of you.'

Buttercup stamped his hoof warningly.

'OK, OK,' Greg said hurriedly. 'The truth is, I'm not a location scout. I'm a night hawker. I travel the world searching for treasure. It's all about finders being keepers.'

'That doesn't sound exactly legal,' Max replied.

His dad shrugged. 'It was never going to be a career that fitted being a father or a husband.'

Max felt like he'd been punched in the stomach. 'You were never going to come back, were you?'

'I wanted to,' his father said. 'I just couldn't.'

'Yes you *could*,' Max said quietly. 'But you chose money over me.'

117

His dad stared up at him. 'I'd have come back to you once I'd sold the elixir. I *can* come back now.' He scrambled to his feet and ran over to the money. He gathered up armfuls of notes and clasped them against his chest.

'You know what I think?' Max said. 'I think that even if you had come back, it wouldn't have been long before you'd have found a reason to leave again. Did you know you haven't once asked me if I've been alright in all the years you've been away, if anything bad had happened, or if David's been treating me OK...'

His voice tailed off as the money on the ground suddenly lifted in the air and whirled around them like it was on a spin cycle. Max's robes whipped about him and Liah leaned against Buttercup to stop herself being blown off her feet. Faster and faster the tornado whirled, until all of the money, including the briefcase was spinning around them.

'No!' shrieked Greg as the wads of money were torn from his hands to join the rest.

Suddenly the money burst into flames and almost instantly turned to ash. The wind disappeared as suddenly as it had arrived leaving small piles of smouldering dust. 'The money,' Greg whimpered. 'It's all gone.' He dropped to his knees, too caught up in his grief over the burned cash to notice he was being observed by a seven-foot-tall skeleton.

Max stared down at his dad. *How did I ever think he was cool?* 'You know,' he said carefully, 'bad things happen in life. What makes you a man is learning to deal with them.'

Death stepped forward. 'It is time,' he boomed. Raising his scythe he cracked the handle into the ground three times. Instantly the whirlwind returned, whipping around the group in a fury.

'Max,' his father cried, his voice sounding more and more distant. 'I'm sorry.'

* * *

Moments later, Liah, Death, Max and Buttercup were standing in Death's throne room, where Mopsus was waiting holding a scroll.

'You did it,' he congratulated Max. 'You destroyed the elixir. I never doubted you.'

'Liah was the one who destroyed it,' Max said, holding back the information that she had, for a short while, been prepared to use it to bring Tom back to life.

Liah shot him a grateful look.

'Yes.' Death sat down on his throne and drummed his fingers against the armrests. 'How exactly did you end up in the Overworld, Liah, when you were supposed to be in the kitchen?'

Liah shifted from one foot to another. 'I, uh...'

'I accidentally left the door open,' Max interrupted. 'She must have gone into the cupboard looking for a mop and come out in Crete. What a shocker! Um. That reminds me – you might want to check the broom cupboard and see if anyone else has ... er ... accidentally got lost in there.'

Mopsus raised his bushy eyebrows. 'Is there something you're not telling us, *assistant*?'

The very picture of innocence, Max shrugged. 'Nothing that I can think of.'

'I think...' Death stood up and walked across to Liah. '...you have served your time in my kitchen.'

Liah's eyes flickered nervously. 'If I'm not going to be in the kitchen then – where am I going to work?'

Death swung his scythe so that the glowing blade rested gently against her chest. 'Many people think they can cheat Death but they never can.' He leaned closer to Liah. 'I always catch up with them. Understand?'

Liah licked her lips nervously. 'I understand,' she whispered.

Max took a step forward. If Death wanted to take Liah's life because the elixir had been used to save her, then he'd have to get past Max first.

A gnarled hand shot out and grasped Max's wrist. 'What are you planning on doing?' Mopsus asked with a maggoty smile. 'Offering to play another game?' He tightened his grip. 'Don't go jumping in with your size fives again.'

'Sixes,' Max whispered.

'Mopsus,' Death said without taking his gaze off Liah.

'Yes Master Reaper?'

'Give the boy his contract.'

Mopsus winked at Max and handed him the scroll. 'Your job here is done. You are free to go.'

Max's spirits soared. Amy was safe, and he could go home! He'd never wanted anything more. Then they plummeted again. He couldn't leave Liah, not without knowing she was safe.

Death held out his hand. 'Give me your robes.'

Slowly Max pulled his robes over his head. He handed them over, along with the whistle, cap and belt.

For a moment he was distracted by a bark and a scrabbling of paws. A familiar-looking dog scampered up, his plumy tail wagging. He grabbed the bottom of Death's robes and tugged on them, making playful growling noises.

'It's Larry's dog!' Max said in surprise. 'What's he doing down here?' Then he noticed that the dog had the same opaque shimmering outline as Tom. 'He's dead?' He looked up in shock. 'How? I thought the elixir brought him back to life?'

'As I said,' the Grim Reaper intoned. 'Death cannot be cheated.' He let his hand rest briefly on the dog's head. 'And I rather fancied a one-headed dog to keep me company.'

He stepped towards Liah. Her eyes widened as he stretched out his hands. 'Take them.' He nodded at the robes.

'You want me to p-p-put them back in the catacombs?' she stammered.

'I want you to put them on. I'm in need of a new assistant. Mopsus has decided he has something of a knack for haute cuisine and will take over the kitchen. He has resigned as my personal assistant.'

Liah's mouth opened. 'You want me to be your assistant? I thought…'

'I know what you thought. Would you prefer to join your fiancé?'

'Ex-fiancé.' Liah tossed her hair over her shoulder.

'Ah yes, your ex-fiancé. Your second task will

123

be to extricate him from the broom cupboard and escort him back to where he belongs.'

'And my first task?' Liah asked.

Death glanced at Max. 'To take this young man back to where *he* belongs.'

* * *

Max looked at the light spilling from the living room window. Through a chink in the curtains he could see his mother kneeling by the Christmas tree. She took a brightly wrapped parcel and handed it to Amy who was sitting alongside David on the sofa.

It's Christmas Day! He longed to be in there with them, to be a part of it all, rather than an outsider with his nose pressed up against a pane of freezing glass.

'Well, I guess this is goodbye,' Liah said.

Max nodded. 'So, Death's assistant huh?'

'Yeah.' Liah plucked at her robes. 'Although these are going to have to go. I don't care if wearing them gives me authority in the Underworld. They clash with my hair and do nothing for my figure.'

Max grinned. 'I'm glad you're not dead.'

'Thanks to you.' Liah suddenly threw her arms around him. 'I hope I don't see you in a very long time,' she whispered. Her eyes looked suspiciously bright as she stepped back and withdrew the key from her pocket. She inserted it into the front door, turned it and stepped through without a backward glance.

The door clicked shut. Max waited a moment before inserting his own key and stepping into the hall. 'I'm back,' he shouted out. 'Mum, Amy, Dav... Dad. I'm home!'

The Twins, the Ghost and the Castle

Paul Mason

"The castle had a secret. They were not alone."

Two abandoned children make their home in
a castle – which is haunted by the Duke of
Wellington! The spook helps them hide from the
castle's caretaker. But when developers want to turn
their home into a spa, everyone who loves the castle
must band together to save the day.

£4.99   ISBN 9781408176269